The Little Red Hen

Retold by Jean Horton Berg

ILLUSTRATED BY MEL PEKARSKY

Reading Consultant: Morton Botel

Follett Publishing Company Chicago·New York

Library of Congress Catalog Card Number: 63-7661

FIFTH PRINTING · TLA 5257

A little red hen had a seed.

"Rat," said the little red hen,
"you are big and you can dig.
Will you help me plant the seed?"

"Not I" said the rat.
"I must go and sit on the hill.
I can't help you plant the seed."

"Cat," said the little red hen,
"you are big and you can dig.
Will you help me plant the seed?"
"Not I," said the cat.
"I must go and hunt catnip.
I can't help you plant the seed."

"Pup," said the little red hen,
"you are big and you can dig.
Will you help me plant the seed?"
"Not I," said the pup.
"I must go and fill my dish.
I can't help you plant the seed."

"Well," said the little red hen.
"Rat can't plant the seed.
Cat can't plant the seed.
And Pup can't plant the seed.
I will plant the seed."
And she did.

The seed puffed up.

And the seed shot up.

"See," said the little red hen,

"the seed is a corn plant."

"Rat," said the little red hen,
"will you help me cut the corn?"
"Not I," said the rat.
"I must go and dust my nest.
I can't help you cut the corn."

"Cat," said the little red hen,
"will you help me cut the corn?"
"Not I," said the cat.
"I must go and mend my mat.
I can't help you cut the corn."

"Pup," said the little red hen,
"will you help me cut the corn?"
"Not I," said the pup.
"I must jump and toss my ball.
I can't help you cut the corn."

"Well," said the little red hen.
"Rat can't cut the corn.
Cat can't cut the corn.
And Pup can't cut the corn.
I will cut the corn."

And she did.

"Rat," said the little red hen,
"will you help me shuck the corn?"
"Not I," said the rat.
"I must run and run and run."

"Cat," said the little red hen,
"will you help me shuck the corn?"
"Not I," said the cat.
"I must run and catch the rat."

"Pup," said the little red hen,
"will you help me shuck the corn?"
"Not I," said the pup.
"I must run and chase the cat."

"Well," said the little red hen.
"Rat can't shuck the corn.
Cat can't shuck the corn.
And Pup can't shuck the corn.
I will shuck the corn."

And she did.

"Rat," said the little red hen,
"will you help me cook the corn?"
"Not I," said the rat.
"I'm hot. I must rest in my nest."

"Cat," said the little red hen,
"will you help me cook the corn?"
"Not I," said the cat.
"I'm hot. I must sit on my mat."

"Pup," said the little red hen,
"will you help me cook the corn?"
"Not I," said the pup.
"I'm hot. I must sip from my dish."

"Well," said the little red hen.
"Rat can't cook the corn.
Cat can't cook the corn.
And Pup can't cook the corn.
I will cook the corn."
And she did.

The little red hen said,
"*M–m–m–m–m–m–m–m–m–m!*
The corn is cooked."

The rat said, "*M–m–m–m–m–m!*
I will help you eat it."

The cat said, "*M–m–m–m–m–m!*
I will help you eat it."

The pup said, "*M–m–m–m–m–m!*
I will help you eat it."

The little red hen said,
"You did not help me plant the corn.
You did not help me cut the corn.
You did not help me shuck the corn.
You did not help me cook the corn.
And you shall not help me eat the corn.

"I shall eat the corn,"
said the little red hen.

And she did!

THE LITTLE RED HEN

Reading Level: Level One. *The Little Red Hen* has a total vocabulary of 65 words.

Uses of This Book: Reading for fun. Helping others is emphasized, and children will be amused by the problems the hen has getting her friends to help her.

Word List

All of the 65 words used in *The Little Red Hen* are listed. Regular plurals (*-s*) and regular verb forms (*-s, -ed, -ing*) of words already on the list are not listed separately, but the endings are given in parentheses after the word.

7	a	and		on
	little	can		hill
	red	dig		can't
	hen	will		
	had	help	8	cat
	seed	me		hunt
	rat	plant		catnip
	said	not		
	the		9	pup
	you	I		fill
	are	must		my
	big	go		dish
		sit		

10   well
      she
      did

11   puffed
      up
      shot
      see
      is
      corn

12   cut
      dust
      nest

13   mend
      mat

14   jump
      toss
      ball

16   shuck
      run

17   catch

18   chase

20   cook (ed)
      I'm
      hot
      rest
      in

22   sip
      from

24   eat
      it

25   shall

The Follett BEGINNING-TO-READ Books

Purpose of the Beginning-to-Read Books: To provide easy-to-read materials that will appeal to the interests of primary children. Careful attention is given to vocabulary load and sentence length, but the first criterion is interest to children.

Reading Levels: These books are written at three reading levels, indicated by one, two, or three dots beneath the *Beginning-to-Read* symbol on the back cover. *Level One* books can be read by first grade children in the last half of the school year. As children increase their reading ability they will be able to enjoy *Level Two* books. And as they grow further in their reading ability they will progress to *Level Three* books. Some first grade children will read *Level Two* and *Level Three* books. Many third graders, and even some fourth graders, will read and enjoy *Level One* and *Level Two* books, as well as *Level Three* books. The range of interest of *Beginning-to-Read* books stretches far beyond their reading level.

Use of the Beginning-to-Read Books: Because of their high interest and readability, these books are ideal for independent reading by primary children—at school, in the library, and at home. The books may also be incorporated into the basic reading program to develop children's interests, expand their vocabularies, and improve word-attack skills. It has been suggested that they might serve as the foundation for a skillfully directed reading program. Many *Beginning-to-Read* books correlate with the social studies, science, and other subject fields. All will help children grow in the language arts. Children will read the *Beginning-to-Read* books with confidence, with success, and with real enjoyment.